The Prince

Niccolò Machiavelli

Translated by
Stephen J. Milner

A Phoenix Paperback

First published in Everyman in 1995

J. M. Dent
A division of Orion Books Ltd
Orion House, 5 Upper St Martin's Lane, London WC2H 9EA

This abridged edition, published in 1996 by Phoenix, contains chapters
15 to 26 of *The Prince* by Niccolò Machiavelli

ISBN 1 85799 535 X

Typeset by CentraCet Ltd, Cambridge
Printed in Great Britain by
Clays Ltd, St Ives plc

I

On the Things for which Men, and especially Princes, are Praised or Blamed
(*De his rebus quibus homines et praesertim principes laudantur aut vituperantur*)

It now remains to consider the procedures and policies a prince should adopt in relation to both his subjects and allies. And since I am aware that many have written on this theme, I am afraid that, in also writing about it myself, I may be considered presumptuous, especially as I depart from the methods adopted by others when discussing this subject. But since my intention is to write something useful for the understanding reader, it seems to me more beneficial to go behind to the effectual truth of the matter, rather than focusing on the imagining of it. For many writers have depicted their own republics and principalities which have never been seen or known actually to exist. And since the distance between how one lives and how one should live is so great, he who discards what he does for what he should do, usually learns how to ruin rather than maintain himself. For a man who wants to make a career of doing good in all spheres will be ruined amongst so many who are not good. Therefore, it is necessary for a prince, if he wants to maintain his position, to develop the ability to be not good, and use or not use this ability as necessity dictates.

Leaving aside the imagined aspects of a prince, therefore, and discussing those that are real, I maintain that all men, when they are talked about, and especially princes, since they are more exposed, are remarked upon for various qualities which bring them either praise or blame. For some are considered generous, others miserly (to use a Tuscan term, since avaricious, in our tongue, still refers to someone who desires to possess something by force, whilst we call somebody who refrains from using his own things miserly). Some are considered benefactors, others greedy; some cruel, others merciful; some faithless, others trustworthy; some effeminate and weak, others fierce and bold; some humane, others proud; some lascivious, others chaste; some upright, others cunning; some severe, others easy-going; some serious, others light-hearted; some religious, others sceptical and so on. I realise that everyone will admit that it would be most laudable to find all the good qualities mentioned above combined in a prince. But since it is not possible either to possess or wholly to observe them, because human nature does not allow it, it is necessary for him to be sufficiently prudent that he knows how to avoid the infamy of those vices that will deprive him of his state, and, if at all possible, be wary of those that are less threatening. If this is impossible, however, he should not worry unduly about the latter. Moreover, he should not worry about the infamy incurred by those vices which are indispensable in maintaining his state, because if he examines everything carefully, he will find that something which seems virtue [*virtù*] can, if put into practice, cause his ruin, while another thing which seems a vice can, when put into practice, result in his security and well-being.

II

On Generosity and Meanness
(*De liberalitate et parsimonia*)

Let me begin, therefore, with the first of the qualities mentioned above. I maintain that it would be good to be considered generous. Nevertheless, generosity, when used in such a way as to gain you that 3 reputation, will damage you. Because if it is used virtuously and as it should be used, it is not recognised, and you will not avoid the infamy of its opposite. Therefore, if you want to establish a name for yourself as a generous person, you cannot afford to neglect any kind of lavishness. A prince who acts this way will soon use up all his resources and will eventually, if he wishes to maintain a name for being generous, be constrained to impose extra taxes in addition to the normal levies, and be rigorous and do all he can to acquire money. This will begin to make him odious to the people, and little esteemed on account of his poverty. Consequently, having harmed the majority and rewarded few with his generosity, he will feel the effect of difficulties immediately and be endangered by the first threats that arise. When he realises this and seeks to exercise restraint, he will instantly acquire the reputation of a miser.

Therefore, as a prince cannot employ and gain a reputation for this virtue [*virtù*] of generosity without damaging his position, he should not mind, if he is a prudent man, being called a miser. With the passage of time he will be considered increasingly generous, and given that his income from taxes will be sufficient for him, due to his parsimony, he will be able to defend himself against those who declare war on him, and to launch campaigns without burdening the people with taxes. Consequently, he displays generosity to all those from whom he takes nothing, who are countless in number, and miserliness to all those to whom he gives nothing, who are few. In our own times we have seen great things achieved only by those who have been held miserly. The others have been wiped out. Pope Julius II, who used his reputation for generosity to accede to the Papacy, did not consider keeping it up later, since he wanted to be capable of fighting wars. The current King of France has waged many wars without levying any additional taxes on his subjects, solely because his enduring parsimony has underwritten the extra expenditure. The current King of Spain would not have launched, or won, so many expeditions if he had been reputed generous.

A prince, therefore, should give little thought to being considered miserly if it means not robbing his subjects, being able to defend himself, not becoming impoverished and contemptible, and not being forced to become rapacious. For this is one of those vices which enables him to rule. If anyone should say, 'Caesar rose to power through generosity, and many others have reached the highest positions because they were considered, and were, generous', I would reply, 'You are either a prince already, or you are in the process of becoming a prince. In the first instance this kind of generosity is harmful, in the second it is necessary to be considered generous. Caesar was one of those who wanted to become ruler of Rome, but if, having arrived at that position, he had survived and not tempered his spending, he would have destroyed that power.' And if anyone should answer, 'There have been many princes who have achieved great things with their armies and been held generous', I would reply, 'The prince either spends what is his own and his subjects', or what belongs to others. In the first instance he should be thrifty, in the second unsparing in his generosity. The prince who accompanies his armies, and who lives off plunder, pillage and ransoms, uses what belongs to others. It is necessary for him to be generous, otherwise he would not be followed by his troops. For he can be a more munificent benefactor when handling what does not belong to himself or his subjects, as Cyrus, Caesar and Alexander were. Because disposing of what belongs to others does not diminish your standing but adds to it. Dispensing with what belongs to yourself is the only thing which will harm you, for there is nothing more self-destructive than generosity, because as you practise it you lose the ability to practise it, and become

6
either impoverished and contemptible or, in order to

avoid poverty, rapacious and odious. Being thought contemptible and odious are amongst the things a prince should guard against, and generosity can lead to both the one and the other.' It is wiser, therefore, to be reputed miserly, which breeds infamy but not hatred, than, in seeking to be held generous, being forced to gain a reputation for rapacity, which breeds infamy combined with hate.

III

On Cruelty and Mercy; and Whether it is Better to be Loved than Feared, or the Reverse (*De crudelitate et pietate; et an sit melius amari quam timeri, vel e contra*)

Passing down the list of the aforementioned qualities, I maintain that each prince should desire to be thought merciful and not cruel. Nonetheless, he should be careful not to misuse this mercy. Cesare Borgia was considered cruel, nevertheless his cruelty put the Romagna in order, uniting it and reducing it to peace and loyalty. If one examines this carefully, you will see that he was far more merciful than the Florentine people, who, rather than be thought cruel, let Pistoia destroy itself. A prince, therefore, should pay no heed to the infamy of being considered cruel if it means he keeps his subjects united and loyal. For he will be more merciful by making an example of one or two people than those who allow disorders to continue, resulting in murders and theft due to misjudged mercy. For these disorders usually harm the whole community, whilst the executions a prince orders harm only a single person. The new prince, above all other princes, cannot avoid a reputation for cruelty, since new states are full of dangers. Virgil says in the following words of Dido,

> difficult circumstances and the newness of my kingdom constrain me to undertake these things, and defend my frontiers everywhere with guards.

Nonetheless, he should be circumspect in believing and acting, and not be afraid of his own shadow, proceeding in a manner tempered by prudence and humanity, so that over-confidence does not make him hasty, or excessive mistrust render him intolerable.

This gives rise to an argument: whether it is better to be loved than feared, or the opposite. The answer is that one would like to be both, but since it is difficult to combine the two it is much safer to be feared than loved, if one of the two has to make way. For generally speaking, one can say the following about men: they are ungrateful, inconstant, feigners and dissimulators, avoiders of dangers, eager for gain, and whilst it profits them they are all yours. They will offer you their blood, their property, their life and their offspring when your need for them is remote, as mentioned above. But when your needs are pressing, they turn away. The prince who depends entirely on their words perishes when he finds he has not taken any other precautions. This is because the friendships that are purchased with money and not by greatness and nobility of spirit are paid for, but not collected, and when you need them they cannot be used. Men are less worried about harming somebody who makes himself loved than someone who makes himself feared, for love is held by a chain of obligation which, since men are bad, is broken at every opportunity for personal gain. Fear, on the other hand, is maintained by a dread of punishment which will never desert you.

Nonetheless, the prince should make himself feared in such a way that, even if he is not loved, he avoids being hated, since being feared and not hated can easily go together. This will always happen if he abstains from the property of his subjects and citizens, and from their womenfolk. If he should need to take anyone's life, he should do it when there is a suitable justification and a demonstrable cause. But above all, he should abstain from others' property, since men forget their father's death more quickly than the loss of their patrimony. Moreover, there is never a shortage of reasons for taking property, and the prince who begins to live by robbery finds reasons to sequester what belongs to others. With executions it is the opposite, reasons are more exceptional and less numerous.

But when the prince is with his armies and in charge of a large number of soldiers, then it is very necessary that he does not worry about a reputation for cruelty. Amongst Hannibal's admirable actions is the following: that having led an incredibly large army, made up of countless different races, on campaigns in foreign lands, no dissension ever arose either among the troops themselves or against their leader, irrespective of whether they enjoyed good or bad fortune. This came about for no other reason than his inhuman cruelty, which, together with his other infinite abilities [*virtù*], made him respected and feared in the eyes of his soldiers. Without it, and the effect it had, his other abilities [*virtù*] would not have been enough. The historians, paying scant attention to the matter, on the one hand admire his achievement whilst simultaneously condemning its main cause.

The truth of the assertion that his other abilities [*virtù*] would not have been enough, is seen in the case of Scipio, a man not only exceptional in his own time but also in the annals of all that is known, for his armies rebelled against him in Spain. This happened solely on account of his excessive mercy, which granted more licence to his soldiers than is fitting for military discipline. He was reproached for this in the Senate by Fabius Maximus, who called him the corrupter of the Roman legions. Scipio failed to ensure that the people of Locri were avenged after they had been plundered by one of his legates, nor was the legate in question punished for his insubordination. All this happened due to his accommodating nature. So much so that when some sought to excuse him before the Senate, they noted that many men knew better how not to err than how to punish those who erred. Scipio's nature would, in time, have ruined his fame and glory if he had continued acting this way during his rule. But when he lived under the rule of the Senate, this harmful quality of his remained not only hidden, but even brought him glory.

Returning, therefore, to the subject of being feared or loved, I conclude that since men are loving when it suits them and fearful when it suits the prince, a wise prince should base himself on what is his, not on what belongs to others. He should merely seek, as I said, to avoid hatred.

IV

Whether Princes Should Keep Their Word
(*Quomodo fides a principibus sit servanda*)

Everyone understands how laudable it is for a prince to keep his word and live with integrity and not cunning. Nonetheless, experience shows that nowadays those princes who have accomplished great things have had little respect for keeping their word and have known how to confuse men's minds with cunning. In the end they have overcome those who have preferred honesty.

You must understand, therefore, that there are two ways of fighting: the first using laws, the second force. The first belongs to man, the second to animals. But since the first is often not enough, one must have recourse to the second. It is therefore necessary for a prince to know how to make good use of the animal and the human. This precept was taught to princes by the ancients under the cover of allegory. They wrote

how Achilles and many more of those ancient princes

were entrusted to Chiron the centaur for their upbringing, so that they could be looked after under his tutelage. Having a half-man, half-beast as a teacher simply means that a prince needs to know how to use both natures, for the one without the other does not last.

As it is necessary for a prince to know how to use the animal, therefore, he should choose the fox and the lion from amongst their ranks, since the lion cannot defend itself from traps and the fox cannot defend itself from the wolves. One needs to be a fox, therefore, to recognise traps, and a lion to frighten the wolves. Those who rely simply on the lion do not understand this. A prudent ruler, therefore, cannot, and should not, keep his word when keeping it is to his disadvantage, and when the reasons that made him promise no longer exist. For if all men were good, this precept would not hold good, but since they are bad and would not keep their word to you, you do not have to keep yours to them. Nor is there ever a shortage of legitimate reasons to disguise your disregard. Countless current examples could be cited of this, showing how many peaces, how many promises have been rendered null and void through the untrustworthiness of princes. The one who has known how best to use the fox has come off best. But it is necessary to know how to disguise this nature well and be a great feigner and dissimulator. Men are so simple and so obedient to present needs, that he who deceives will always find people who will let themselves be deceived.

Of the recent examples, I would like to mention one in particular. Alexander VI never did anything, nor thought of anything, apart from deceiving men, and he always found a subject who would enable him to do it. Never was there a man more effective in swearing, who affirmed things with such heavy oaths, and yet stuck to them less. Nonetheless, his deceptions always worked out as he hoped, because he well understood this aspect of life.

It is unnecessary, therefore, for a prince actually to have all the qualities mentioned above, but it is more than necessary to seem to have them. Indeed, I will hazard to say this: that when you have them and when you always keep to them they are harmful, but when you seem to have them they are useful, like seeming merciful, loyal, humane, upright and religious, and being so. But you must remain mentally prepared, so that when it is necessary not to have these qualities you are able, and know how to assume their opposites. It is essential to realise this: that a prince, and above all a new prince, cannot practise all those things which gain men a reputation for being good, as it is often necessary, in order to keep hold of the state, to act contrary to trust, contrary to charity, contrary to humanity, contrary to religion. It is for that reason that he needs a mind prepared to vary as the winds of fortune and free flow of events dictate, and, as stated above, he should not deviate from good if possible, but know how to act badly when necessary.

A prince should take great care, therefore, that nothing issues from his mouth which is not imbued with the five aforementioned qualities. To see him and hear him, he should seem all-merciful, all-trustworthy, all-integrity, all-humanity, all-religion. Nothing is more important to seem to have than this last quality. Generally speaking, men judge more by the eyes than by the hands, because everybody can see, but only a few can feel. Everyone sees what you seem, few feel what you are like. Those few do not dare stand against the opinion of the many who have the majesty of the state defending them. In the actions of all men, and most of all in princes, where there is no appeal to higher judgement, one looks to the result. A prince should seek to win and keep hold of a state. The means will always be judged honourable and praised by everybody, for the common people are always impressed by how things seem and by the way things turn out, and in the world there is nothing except common people. When the many are comfortably settled, the few will find no way in. A certain current prince, who had better remain anonymous, preaches nothing but peace and trust, and is an implacable enemy of both. If he had observed either of these qualities, he would have lost either his reputation or his state on several occasions.

V

On the Avoidance of Contempt and Hatred
(*De contemptu et odio fugiendo*)

Since the qualities discussed above were only the most important ones, I would like briefly to consider the others under this general heading: that the prince, as hinted at above, should seek to avoid those things that render him odious and contemptible. Whenever he avoids them, he will have fulfilled his job and will find that his other evil actions pose no threat to him at all. As I have said, he will be hated above all if he is rapacious and seizes his subjects' property and women. He should refrain from doing this. The majority of men live happily so long as they are not deprived of either their property or their honour. The prince has only to contend with the ambition of a few which can be easily restrained in a variety of ways. He will be held in contempt if he is considered capricious, superficial, effeminate, cowardly and irresolute. A prince should avoid these things like the plague, and seek to show greatness, courage, gravity and strength in his actions, ensuring that his decisions in his subjects' private affairs are irrevocable and that he maintains such standing that nobody thinks to deceive or outwit him.

The prince who earns this reputation for himself is held in high esteem, and as long as he is understood to be a great man and revered by his subjects, it is difficult to conspire against and attack such a person when they are esteemed. For a prince should have two fears: an internal one, in regard to his subjects, and an external one, in regard to foreign powers. He defends himself against the latter with good arms and good allies, and when he has good arms he will always have good allies. Internal affairs will always remain stable whilst external matters are stable, unless they have already been disturbed by a conspiracy. And even when external circumstances change, if the prince has organised and conducted himself as I have said, and if he does not capitulate, he will always withstand any assault, as did Nabis the Spartan (as I mentioned). As regards his subjects, however, when external circumstances are stable he should be fearful lest they conspire against him. The prince can secure himself against this quite well, by avoiding being hated or despised and ensuring the people are content with him. It is vital to do this, as was made clear at length above. One of the most potent remedies a prince can have against conspiracies is not being hated by the population as a whole, because conspirators always hope to satisfy the people with the death of the prince. When they think they might offend the people, they are not courageous enough to begin such an enterprise, because the difficulties conspirators face are endless. Experience shows that there have been many conspiracies, but that precious few have turned out as planned. For a conspirator cannot act alone, nor can he associate himself with anybody except those he considers dissatisfied, and the instant he discloses his intentions to dissatisfied citizens, he grants them the means of satisfying themselves, for they can obviously then hope for all kinds of rewards. Consequently, any associate must either be an exceptional friend or a steadfast enemy of the prince if he is to keep faith with you, for, whilst informing guarantees profit, co-operation promises nothing but uncertainty and danger.

18 To put it briefly, I maintain that from the conspirator's

standpoint there is nothing but fear, envy and the dreadful possibility of punishment, while the prince has the majesty of being a prince, the laws and the support of his friends and the state on his side, all of which defend him. When the people's goodwill is joined to all these, it is impossible that anyone should be so bold as to conspire. While a conspirator is normally fearful before he carries out the evil deed, in this instance he must also be afraid after he has committed the crime (as he has the people as his enemy), and for this reason he cannot hope to find any refuge.

Endless examples could be cited on this subject, but I will satisfy myself with one in particular which occurred within our fathers' lifetime. Messer Annibale Bentivoglio, grandfather of the present Annibale and ruler of Bologna at that time, was murdered by the Canneschi who had conspired against him. Only messer Giovanni remained of his line, and he was still in swaddling clothes. The people rose up at once, and murdered all the Canneschi. This was due to the popular goodwill in which the Bentivoglio family was held in those days, which was so great that although, with Annibale's death, not one of that family was left in Bologna who could rule the city, the people of Bologna went to Florence to recall a person they heard had been born a Bentivogli. Until that point he had been raised as the son of an artisan. They conferred the government of the city upon him, and he ruled over Bologna until such time as messer Giovanni reached a suitable age for governing.

I conclude, therefore, that a prince should pay scant attention to conspiracies so long as the people are well disposed towards him. But when they are his enemy and hold him in contempt, he must be fearful of everybody and everything. Well-organised states and wise princes have carefully sought not to deprive the nobles of hope and to satisfy the people and keep them happy, for this is one of the most important concerns that a prince has.

Amongst the well-organised and well-governed kingdoms of our own time is France. In it one finds countless good institutions, upon which the king's liberty and security depend. Foremost amongst these is the *parlement* with its authority. The man who established that kingdom recognised the ambition and insolence of the powerful, judging it necessary for them to have a bit placed in their mouths which could be used to control them. He also recognised that the people's hatred for the nobles was based on fear, and in seeking to reassure them he did not want this particular task to fall to the king, in order to save him from the nobles' displeasure should he favour the people, and the people's were he to favour the nobles. Consequently, he established a third party as judge, to beat the great and favour the small without the king being reproached personally. There could not be a better or more prudent institution, nor one more responsible for the security of the king and the kingdom. Another important point can be drawn from this: that princes should ensure that other people administer unpopular measures while the granting of favours remains in their own hands. Once again I conclude that a prince must value the nobles, whilst not making himself hated by the people.

To many people it might seem that an examination of the lives and deaths of certain Roman emperors furnish examples that contradict this opinion of mine, since some lived consistently distinguished lives, demonstrating great strength [*virtù*] of mind, and yet lost the Empire or were even murdered by their own people who conspired against them. As I wish to reply to these objections, I will discuss the qualities of some of these emperors, showing how the reasons for their downfall are not out of keeping with the reasons adduced by me. I will choose for consideration events that are known to those who read about those times. I want all those emperors who succeeded to the Empire between Marcus the philosopher and Maximus to suffice, namely Marcus, Commodus his son, Pertinax, Julian, Severus, Antoninus, Caracalla his son, Macrinus, Heliogabalus, Alexander and Maximinus.

The first thing to note is that whereas in other principalities there was only the ambition of the nobles and the insolence of the people to deal with, the Roman emperors had a third difficulty: they had to tolerate the cruelty and greed of the soldiers. This was so difficult that it caused the ruination of many, as it was hard to satisfy the soldiers and the people. For the people loved peace and consequently loved modest rulers, while the soldiers loved rulers who were military-minded and arrogant, cruel and greedy. They wanted their rulers to demonstrate these qualities on the people, so that they could double their salaries and give vent to their avarice and cruelty.

These considerations meant that those emperors who, either naturally or through their own efforts, lacked a strong reputation which enabled them to hold both parties in check, came to ruin. When the majority of them, and especially those who assumed power as political newcomers, realised the difficulty presented by these two different humours, they preferred to satisfy the soldiers, as they considered damaging the people of little importance. This policy was expedient, for such rulers cannot but be hated by somebody, and should therefore first ensure that they are not hated by everybody. When this proves impossible, they should seek as much as possible to avoid the hatred of the most powerful groups. Therefore, those emperors who needed more than normal levels of support as newcomers more often allied themselves to the soldiers than to the people. Whether or not this was a profitable policy nonetheless depended upon their ability to maintain their standing with the soldiers.

The reasons mentioned above explain why Marcus, Pertinax and Alexander, men who lived modest lives and were humane and kindly, and were lovers of justice and enemies of cruelty, came to unfortunate ends, with the exception of Marcus. He lived and died most honourably only because he succeeded to the Empire by hereditary right and did not owe any debt of obligation for it either to the soldiers or the people. In addition, as he possessed many qualities [*virtù*] that earned him respect, he was able to keep both parties within limits throughout his life, and was never hated nor despised. Pertinax, on the other hand, came to grief at the very outset of his administration, for he was created emperor contrary to the wishes of the soldiers, who were used to living dissolute lives under Commodus and were unable to bear the honest life which Pertinax desired them to follow. For this reason he became hated, a hate which was augmented by the disrespect felt on account of his age.

It should be noted at this point that hatred is felt as a result of both good and evil deeds. However, as I said above, if a prince wants to keep hold of his state he is often forced not to be good, because when the group you judge necessary for your safe-keeping is corrupt, whether it be the people, soldiers or nobles, it is worthwhile adapting to their humour in order to satisfy them. In that instance good works are your enemy. But let us come to Alexander, who was of such goodness that amongst the other praiseworthy things that were attributed to him there is the following: that in the fourteen years he held the empire not one person was put to death without trial. Nonetheless, because he was despised, considered effeminate and seen as a man who allowed himself to be governed by his mother, the army conspired against him and murdered him.

Turning, in contrast, to the qualities of Commodus, Severus, Antonino Caracalla and Maximus: they are seen to have been very cruel and very greedy. For in order to satisfy the soldiers they inflicted every possible kind of injury on the people. All of them except Severus came to unfortunate ends. Severus, however, had such personal ability and strength [*virtù*] that in keeping the soldiers friendly towards him he was always able to reign happily, despite the fact that he oppressed the people. His personal abilities [*virtù*] made him so impressive in the eyes of both the soldiers and the people, that the latter remained dumbfounded and stupefied, and the former respectful and satisfied.

Because his actions were notable and outstanding for a new prince, I want to demonstrate briefly just how well he knew how to use the character of the fox and the lion, whose natures, as I have said, it is necessary for a prince to imitate. As soon as Severus realised the Emperor Julian's indolence, he persuaded his army, which he was leading in Slavonia, that it was right for them to go to Rome and avenge the death of Pertinax, who had been murdered by the Praetorian Guards. Under this pretence he led his army against Rome without disclosing his aspirations to the Empire, and was in Italy before anybody knew he had set out. When he arrived in Rome he was elected Emperor by a terrified Senate, and Julian was killed. After this beginning, Severus faced two remaining difficulties in securing his rule over the whole state. Firstly from Pescennius Niger in Asia, commander of the Asiatic armies, who had declared himself Emperor, and secondly from the West, where Albinus was also aspiring to the Empire. Since he judged it dangerous to declare himself an enemy of both men, he decided to attack Niger and trick Albinus. He wrote to the latter explaining how he had been elected Emperor by the Senate and that he, Severus, wished to share that dignity with Albinus. He sent him the title of Caesar and, with the agreement of the Senate, made him co-Emperor. Albinus accepted these things as true. But once Severus had beaten and killed Niger, and pacified the East he complained in the Senate on his return to Rome that Albinus had sought to murder him despite the benefits Severus had conferred on him. It was therefore necessary for him to go and punish his ingratitude. He then sought him out in France, and took from him both his state and his life.

Whoever examines this man's actions carefully, therefore, will find he was a ferocious lion and a most astute fox, observing also how he was feared and revered by everyone and not hated by the armies. It is not surprising that he was able to hold on to such great power as a newcomer, for his exceptional reputation always defended him from the hatred which his greed aroused in the people. His son Antoninus was also a man who had excellent qualities that rendered him remarkable in the public's view and pleasing to the soldiers. For he was a military man who tolerated all hardships and who despised delicacies and every other kind of effeminacy, something that endeared him to the soldiers. Nonetheless, his ferocity and cruelty were so great and unparalleled (since after countless individual murders he killed a large part of the Roman, and all of Alexandria's, population) that he became universally hated, and even began to be feared by those around him, with the result that he was murdered by a centurion in the midst of his army.

It is worth noting that princes cannot avoid deaths such as these, as they result from the determination of a single-minded will, and anyone who is not himself afraid of death can attack them. A prince need not be too fearful of such a death, however, as they are very rare. He must merely seek not to offend seriously any of those who serve him personally or who surround him in service of the state. This is what Antoninus did, killing a brother of the centurion in an offensive manner, and threatening him daily. However, he kept him in his bodyguard, a decision that was rash and self-destructive, and so it proved.

But let us turn to Commodus, who found it very easy to hold on to the Empire, for being the son of Marcus, he inherited it by right. All he had to do was follow in his father's footsteps and both the soldiers and the people would have been satisfied. But as he was cruel and brutal by nature, he sought to please the armies and make them dissolute in order to practise his rapaciousness on the people. In addition, he did not maintain his dignity, often descending into the arenas to fight the gladiators and do other base things not worthy of his imperial majesty, and so became contemptible in the soldiers' eyes. As he was hated by one side and despised by the other, he was conspired against and killed.

We still have to recount the qualities of Maximinus. He was a most warlike man who was elected Emperor by the armies when they became tired of Alexander's effeminacies, which I mentioned above. He remained Emperor for only a very short time, as two things made him both hated and despised. Firstly, he was of the most lowly birth, having previously been a shepherd in Thrace (a fact that was remarked upon by everybody and meant that he was viewed by everyone with great contempt), and secondly, since at the beginning of his rule he delayed going to Rome to assume the imperial throne, having gained a reputation for himself as being extremely cruel through the actions of his prefects in Rome and elsewhere in the Empire, as both he and the prefects had committed many cruelties. Consequently, driven by the stigma of his lowly birth and by the hatred of his fearful ferocity, the whole world rose up, with Africa rebelling first and then the Senate backed by all the people of Rome, and the whole of Italy conspired against him. His own army also joined them, and while they were besieging Aquileia and experiencing some difficulty in occupying the town they killed him, as they were tired of his cruelty and were less fearful of him once they saw how many enemies he had.

I do not want to discuss Heliogabalus, or Macrinus, or Julian, who were destroyed almost immediately for being generally despised, but come to the conclusion of this discourse. I maintain that nowadays princes less often face the difficulty of having to satisfy the soldiers under their command by extraordinary means, because, despite the fact that they have to bear them in mind to some extent, problems are nonetheless quickly resolved because none of these princes have armies that have grown old alongside the provincial governments and administrations, as was the case with the armies of the Roman Empire. Besides, if it were necessary at that time to satisfy the soldiers more than the people, this was because the soldiers were stronger than the people. Nowadays it is more important for all princes, with the possible exception of the Turk and the Sultan, to satisfy the people more than the soldiers, as the people are more powerful.

I make an exception of the Turk because he always keeps a force of twelve thousand infantry and fifteen thousand cavalry around him, upon which depend both the security and the strength of his realm. It is therefore necessary for that ruler to set aside all other concerns if he wishes to maintain the friendship of the soldiers. Similarly, the Sultan's kingdom is wholly in the hands of the soldiers, and he must maintain their allegiance even at the people's cost. One also has to bear in mind that the Sultan's state is of a different form from all the other principalities, since it is similar to the Christian Papacy, which cannot be termed either an hereditary, or a new, principality. For the state is not inherited by and ruled by the sons of the former prince, but rather by someone elected to that position. Since this is an ancient provision, it cannot be called a new principality because it experiences none of the difficulties of the new ones, for although the prince is new, the institutions of that state are old and formulated to receive him as if he were an hereditary ruler.

But let us return to the matter in hand. I maintain that anyone who considers the above discourse will observe that either hate or contempt have been the cause of the aforementioned emperors' downfalls. He will also realise why it happened that when some emperors proceeded in one way and others differently in each of these groups, one person had a happy and the rest an unhappy ending. For it would have been useless and harmful for Pertinax and Alexander to imitate Marcus, as they were new princes and he was an hereditary prince. Similarly, it would have been harmful for Caracalla, Commodus and Maximus to imitate Severus, as they lacked the necessary personal ability [*virtù*] to follow in his footsteps. A new prince in a new principality, therefore, cannot imitate the actions of Marcus, nor is it necessary for him to follow those of Severus, but he must take those parts that are necessary for the foundation of his state from Severus, and those parts that are fitting and glorious for the conservation of an already established and secure state from Marcus.

VI

Whether Fortresses and Many Other Things Commonly Used by Princes are Useful or Useless
(*An arces et multa alia quae cotidie a principibus fiunt utilia an inutilia sint*)

Some princes, in order to hold on to their states securely, have disarmed their subjects, some have kept their subject towns divided, and some have fostered animosity against themselves. Others, on assuming the state, have sought to win over those they suspected; still others have built fortresses whilst others have ruined and destroyed them. And although one cannot pass a final judgement on any of these policies without examining the particulars of the states where such decisions were made, nonetheless I will discuss the matter in the general terms which seem fitting.

A new prince has never disarmed his subjects. On the contrary, finding them unarmed, he always armed them. For in arming them, they become his arms. Those whom you consider suspect become loyal, those who are loyal remain so, and your subjects become your supporters. And because it is impossible to arm all your subjects, when you favour those you arm, you can deal more securely with the others, for those you arm recognise the difference in the way you treat them, and this binds them to you more strongly. The others will excuse you, judging it necessary that those who face greater danger and are more at your disposal are treated more favourably. But when you disarm them, you start to offend them, for in doing so you demonstrate your distrust of them, either because of their cowardice or disloyalty. Both of these opinions will result in your being hated. Since you cannot remain unarmed, you are compelled to turn to mercenary troops, the characteristics of which are as noted above. No matter how good these troops are, they cannot be strong enough to defend you from powerful enemies and suspect subjects. Therefore, as I said, a new prince in a new principality has always organised military matters there, and examples of this are widespread in the histories.

But when a prince acquires a new state which he joins to his old one like a limb, it is then necessary for him to disarm that state, with the exception of those who were his supporters in acquiring it. In time, it is even necessary to mollify and emasculate these supporters when the opportunities arise, organising himself so that all the weapons in the state are in the hands of his own troops who were used to living by his side in the old state.

Our ancestors and those who were considered wise used to claim that it was necessary to hold Pistoia with factions and Pisa with fortresses, and consequently nurtured differences in several subject cities in order to keep hold of them more securely. This policy must have been a good one during the times when Italy was, to a certain extent, balanced. But I do not think it can be considered a good maxim these days, as I do not believe that divisions ever do anybody any good. On the contrary, necessity dictates that when divided cities are approached by the enemy they are lost almost immediately, for the weaker faction will always adhere to the external forces, and the other faction will not be able to resist.

In my opinion, the Venetians, motivated by the reasons given above, nurtured the Guelf and Ghibelline factions in their subject cities, and although they never let it lead to bloodshed, they nevertheless fostered disagreements between them so that, bound up in their differences, those citizens would not unite against Venice. That this did not subsequently turn out as planned is clear, for when they were routed at Vailà one of the factions there took courage, and seized the whole state from them. Such policies, therefore, suggest weakness in the prince, since a bold prince would never allow such divisions, for they are profitable only in times of peace when he can use them to govern his subjects more easily. When war comes, however, the weakness of such policies is exposed.

There is no doubting that princes become great when they overcome difficulties and obstacles that are placed in their way. Fortune, therefore, especially when she wants to make a new prince great (and new princes have more need to acquire reputation than hereditary ones), creates enemies and has them launch campaigns against such princes, so that they have to overcome them, thereby climbing higher up the ladders that their enemies have provided for them. Consequently, many consider that a new prince, when he has the chance, should cunningly nurture some opposition, so that in overcoming it there is a subsequent increase in his standing.

Princes, and especially new ones, have found those men who were considered dangerous at the beginning of their rule more loyal and more useful than those who were initially trusted. Pandolfo Petrucci, the ruler of Siena, managed his state more with the help of those he had feared than with anyone else. But one cannot generalise about this matter, as it varies according to circumstance. But I will say this: those men who were enemies of the prince at the beginning of a principality, and who need somebody to rely on to maintain their own positions, are always easily won over by the prince. And the extent to which they are compelled to serve him loyally is in proportion to their need to erase the unfavourable impression the prince had formed of them by their actions. In this way the prince will always derive more profit from them than from those who in serving him too faithfully neglect his affairs.

Since the subject demands it, I do not want to fail to

remind princes who have acquired states with the backing of insiders to ponder at length the reasons that have motivated those who lent their support. If it is not natural affection for the prince but solely disaffection with the previous state, the prince will maintain their friendship only with the greatest of effort and difficulty, as it is impossible for him to satisfy them. When he considers the reason for this thoroughly, examining ancient and recent examples, he will note that those men who were content with the previous state are much more easily won over as friends, even though they were formerly his enemies, than those who, not being content with it, became his allies and backed him in its occupation.

Princes, in order to hold their states more firmly, have traditionally built fortresses to act as a bridle and bit on those who might conspire against them and as a safe refuge from any sudden attack. I applaud this policy, because it has been used since ancient times. Nonetheless, in our own times messer Niccolo Vitelli was seen to destroy two fortresses in Città di Castello in order to keep hold of that state. When Guidobaldo, the Duke of Urbino, returned to his dominion, from which he had been expelled by Cesare Borgia, he razed to the ground all the fortresses of the province, thinking this would subsequently make it more difficult to lose that state. When the Bentivogli returned to Bologna they followed a similar course of action. Fortresses, therefore, are useful or not, depending upon the situation at the time, and if they benefit you in one way they harm you in another. You can summarise the matter as follows: the prince who fears the people more than outsiders should build fortresses, but the prince who fears outsiders more than the people should ignore them. The castle which Francesco Sforza built at Milan has caused, and will cause, more trouble to the Sforza household than any other source of disorder in that state. The best kind of fortress, however, is not to be hated by the people. Because even though you have fortresses, if the people hate you they will not save you, for there is never a shortage of outsiders ready to help the people when they take up arms. In our own times there are no examples of fortresses benefiting a ruler, except for the Countess of Forlì when her husband Count Girolamo was killed, because thanks to the castle she was able to resist the popular onslaught and wait for support from Milan and then re-establish her position. At that time circumstances were such that outsiders were unable to aid the people. The fortresses were later of little use to her when Cesare Borgia attacked her and the people joined with him, as an outsider, against her. In the long run, therefore, she would have been safer not being hated by the people than having fortresses.

All things considered, therefore, I am prepared to praise princes who build fortresses and princes who do not, and blame anyone who places their trust in fortresses and considers being hated by the people of little importance.

VII

How a Prince Should Act in Order to Gain Reputation
(*Quod principem deceat ut egregius habeatur*)

Nothing makes a prince more highly esteemed than the assumption of great undertakings and striking examples of his own ability. In our own times we have Ferdinand of Aragon, the current King of Spain. He can almost be called a new prince, as he has risen from being ruler of a small kingdom, through fame and glory, to be the foremost King in Christendom. If you consider his actions, you will see that they were all magnificent and some of them exceptional. At the beginning of his reign he attacked Granada, and the 38 campaign provided the basis of his power. First, he launched it when he was undisturbed and had no fear of being obstructed, keeping the minds of the barons of Castile occupied, so that in concentrating on the war they did not think of making political changes. In the meantime he was acquiring reputation and authority over them without their realising it. He was also able to establish armies with money from the Church and the people and, during the long war, he laid the foundations for his own military force which has subsequently brought him honour. In addition, to enable him to engage in more extensive campaigns, always under the cover of religion, he has employed a pious cruelty in tracking down and driving the Mariscos out of his kingdom, an example which could not have been more pitiful and extraordinary. He attacked Africa under this same cloak of religion, launched the campaign in Italy, and recently assaulted France. He has always, therefore, performed and planned great schemes, which have always kept his subjects guessing and astonished, awaiting their outcome. And these feats of his have always followed hard on each other's heels, in such a way that people have never had the space to conspire quietly against him.

It is also quite profitable for a prince to give striking examples of his character in matters of internal government, like those recounted about messer

Bernabò of Milan. For, when someone does something extraordinary in civic life, be it good or bad, the prince can reward or punish them in such a way that it causes considerable discussion. Above all a prince should operate to secure a reputation for himself as a great man and a keen intellect in all he does.

A prince gains a greater reputation when he is either a true friend or a mortal enemy, namely when he backs one side against another without hesitation. This policy is always more useful than remaining neutral, since if two of his neighbours who are powerful rulers come to blows, they are either of a kind that will cause him to be fearful if they win or they are not. In either of these cases, it will be more profitable for him to declare his allegiances and enter into a genuine war. Because in the first instance, if he does not declare himself, he will always be at the mercy of the victor, much to the pleasure and satisfaction of the vanquished party. In addition, there will be nobody who will protect him or provide him with refuge, because the winner does not want suspect allies who will not help him in times of adversity. The loser will not receive him, as he was unwilling to take his chance with the eventual loser in armed combat.

Antiochus invaded Greece at the invitation of the

Aetolians as they wanted him to drive the Romans out. He sent orators to the Achaeans, who were allies of the Romans, requesting they remain neutral. The Romans, on the other hand, were seeking to persuade them to take up arms on their behalf. The subject was presented for discussion in the Achaean council, where the orator sent by Antiochus persuaded them to remain neutral. The Roman legate replied to this decision as follows: 'Nothing is further from your interests than what they say about your non-intervention in the war, for you will be the victor's prize, without favour and without dignity.'

It will always be the case that the person who is not your friend will seek your neutrality, while your friend will ask you to declare your armed support. Irresolute princes, in order to avoid current difficulties, normally assume the path of neutrality and are normally ruined as a result. But when you boldly declare your support for one side, if the person you back wins, although he is powerful and you are at his mercy, he is indebted to you and there is a bond of mutual support. In such instances, men are never so dishonest that they would crush you in a shocking display of ingratitude. Moreover, victories are never so clear-cut that the victors can ignore all considerations, especially as regards justice. But if the person you back loses, he will grant you refuge, and in helping you as much as he can, your shared fortunes may improve.

In the second case, when the combatants are such that you have no cause to fear the winner, it is even more prudent to commit yourself, for you help somebody ruin someone else. If your ally is wise he should be saving his opponent. For when he wins, he is at your mercy, and, with your backing, it is impossible for him to lose.

It should be noted at this point that a prince should never join forces with somebody more powerful than himself to attack another, unless he is compelled by necessity, as stated above, because when he wins he become a prisoner. Princes should avoid, as much as possible, being subject to another's will. The Venetians allied themselves with the French against the Duke of Milan. They could have avoided that alliance which led to their ruin. But when it is unavoidable (as it was for the Florentines when the Pope and Spain moved with their armies to attack Lombardy), then the prince should commit himself for the reasons mentioned above. No state should ever think it can always make secure decisions. On the contrary, it should consider all decisions it takes as risks, because it is in the nature of things that in seeking to avoid one difficulty you run into another. Prudence lies in understanding the nature of the difficulties, and taking the least problematic as best.

A prince should also demonstrate that he admires the virtues [*virtù*] of other people, encouraging men with ability [*virtù*], and honouring those who excel in a particular field. Similarly, he should encourage his citizens to believe that they can go about their business undisturbed, whether it be trading, agriculture or any other profession, so that one man is not afraid to increase his wealth for fear that it might be taken from him, and another is not afraid to start a business for fear of excessive taxes. For a prince should prepare rewards for those who want to do these things, or for anyone who thinks of any way to make his city or state greater. In addition, at the appropriate times of the year, he should entertain the people with celebrations and performances. And since all cities are divided into guilds or family groups he should bear these groups in mind, meeting with them periodically, showing himself to be humane and munificent whilst, nonetheless, always firmly retaining the majesty of his position, for this must be maintained at all times.

VIII

On the Secretaries Who Accompany the Prince
(De his quos a secretis principes habent)

The choice of ministers is a task of no little importance for a prince. Whether they are good or not depends upon the prudence of the prince. The first impression one forms of a ruler's intelligence is based on an examination of the men he keeps around him. When they are capable and loyal, he can always be thought wise because he recognises them as capable and keeps them loyal. When they are otherwise it always gives a bad impression, since the first mistake he makes, he makes in this choice.

Nobody who knew messer Antonio da Venafro as the minister of Pandolfo Petrucci, prince of Siena, could help considering Pandolfo a most valiant person in having such a man as his minister. For there are three types of intelligence: the first understands by itself, the second perceives what others understand, and the third does not understand by itself or with the help of others. The first is most excellent, the second good and the third useless. This necessarily meant that if Pandolfo was not in the first rank he was at least in the second. For whenever a prince has the ability to recognise the good or the bad that a person says or does (even if that person has no inventive spirit of his own), the prince can identify the bad and good works of the minister, praise the latter and punish the former. The minister cannot hope to deceive him, and consequently he continues to behave fittingly.

There is one infallible way, however, that you can recognise the character of a minister. When you notice that the minister is more concerned with himself than with you, and that he seeks his own profit in all he does, such a person will never make a good minister, nor can you ever trust him. For the man who handles a state ruled by one person should never think of himself but always of the prince, and not bring anything to his prince's attention that does not concern him. For his part, the prince should consider the minister's needs in order to keep him loyal. He should honour him, make him rich, bind him with obligations, and include him in the distribution of honours and positions so that he sees that he cannot exist without the prince. In this way the many honours he has received do not make him desire more honours, the great riches do not make him desire more riches, and the many positions make him fearful of political changes. When ministers relate to their princes like this, and likewise princes to their ministers, there is mutual trust between them. When this does not happen, the result is always harmful for both parties.

IX

How Flatterers are Avoided
(*Quomodo adulatores sint fugiendi*)

I do not want to leave aside an important matter, a mistake that it is easy for a prince to make unless he is very prudent and has good judgement. This concerns flatterers, of which the courts are full, for men become so obsessed with their own affairs, deceiving themselves in the process, that it is difficult to defend themselves from this plague. In seeking to combat it, one runs the risk of becoming hated. There is no other defence against flattery than letting men know that they do not offend you by telling you the truth. But when everybody feels able to tell you the truth, you lose respect. A prince should therefore follow a third path, choosing wise men in his state who alone are given the freedom to speak to him truthfully, and only about those things he asks and nothing else. But he should consult them on all matters, and listen to their views, only then deciding on his own, as he sees fit. He should also comport himself with each of these advisers in such a way that each knows that the more freely he speaks the more readily he will be accepted. He should not listen to anyone except these few; he should follow up what has been decided and be resolute in his decisions. Anyone who acts differently either comes to grief amongst flatterers or changes his mind regularly because of the variety of opinions. This gives rise to his being held in little esteem.

Whilst on the subject, I want to cite a modern example. Father Luca, agent of Maximilian, the current Emperor, when speaking of His Majesty, reported how he never consulted with anybody, and nothing turned out as he planned. This was because he followed the opposite course to the one laid out above. For the Emperor is a secretive man who does not communicate his plans to anyone, nor does he take advice. But when put into action, these are gradually revealed and disclosed, and begin to be opposed by those who are around him, and because he is compliant he is dissuaded from pursuing them. Consequently, what is achieved one day is destroyed the next, nobody ever understands what he wants or plans to do, and they cannot rely on his decisions.

A prince, therefore, should always seek advice, but when he wants to and not when others see fit. Indeed, he should discourage people from advising him on anything, unless asked by him. However, he should be a keen and general enquirer, and then a patient listener to the truth concerning the matters he has asked about. Moreover, should he find anyone reluctant to tell him the truth for whatever reason, he should become angry. There is a widespread belief that some princes who have a reputation for being prudent in fact owe that reputation not to their own natural abilities but to the quality of the advice at their disposal. But this belief is quite unfounded. The following general rule is infallible: that a prince who himself is not wise cannot be well advised, unless by chance he should place himself in the hands of a most prudent man who manages all his affairs. In this case he might be well advised, but he would not last long, as the man who governs on his behalf would seize the state from him in no time. But when a prince who is not wise seeks advice from more than one person, he will never have a consensus of views, nor will he know how to establish one himself. Each of the advisers will consider their own concerns, and the prince will not know either how to punish such advisers or even to recognise them. They cannot be otherwise, for you will find that men always prove evil unless a particular need forces them to be good. So the conclusion must be that good advice, whoever gives it, had better arise from the prudence of the prince, rather than the prudence of the prince from the good advice.

X

Why the Princes of Italy have Lost their States
(*Cur italiae principes regnum amiserunt*)

The above-mentioned things, if prudently executed, make a new prince seem long established, rendering him instantly more secure and more stable in the state, as if he had been there for a long time. For the actions of a new prince are under far more scrutiny than those of an hereditary one. And when those actions are recognised as virtuous, they captivate men far more, and bind them to him far tighter, than ancient blood. For men are much more taken by present things than past ones, and when they find the present to their liking they enjoy it and do not look for anything else. Indeed, they will defend him on all accounts, so long as he himself is not lacking in other respects. In this way he will enjoy twice the glory, having given life to a new principality and furnished it and strengthened it with new laws, strong arms and good examples.

Similarly, a man who is born a prince and loses it through his lack of prudence incurs twice the shame.

If the rulers of our own time in Italy who have lost their states are considered – for example the King of Naples, the Duke of Milan and others, it is found they share a weakness, first of all in arms, for the reasons already discussed at length. Secondly, some of them had the people as enemies, or even if they had the people as friends, they did not know how to secure themselves against the nobles. For without these weaknesses states that are sufficiently strong to keep an army in the field are not lost. Philip of Macedon (not Alexander's father but the one defeated by Titus Quintius) possessed a small state in comparison with the power of the Romans and Greeks who attacked him. Nonetheless, because he was a military man who knew how to win over the people and secure himself against the nobles, he sustained the war against them for many years. And if he eventually lost his rule over a few cities, the kingdom nevertheless remained his own.

So these princes of ours who have held their principalities for many years only to then lose them, should not blame fortune but rather their own indolence, because having never thought that quiet times might change (a weakness shared by many men who fail to consider the possibility of a storm when times are calm) when the adverse weather then arrives, they think only of fleeing and not of defending themselves. They hope that the people, when they grow tired of the arrogance of the victors, will recall them. This policy is a good one when all else fails, but it is a very bad policy to abandon all others to follow this one. For one should never fall, believing someone will be found to gather one up. This either does not happen, or, if it does happen, it is not safe, as this kind of defence is cowardly and not dependent upon oneself. And the only defences that are good, that are certain and that are durable are those which depend solely on oneself and on one's own strength and ability [*virtù*].

XI

How Much Fortune can Influence Human Affairs, and How She Should be Resisted
(*Quantum fortuna in rebus humanis possit, et quomodo illi sit occurrendum*)

I am not unaware that many were, and still are of the opinion that human affairs are so governed by fortune and God that man is incapable of managing them with his prudence, indeed, that man has no remedy at all. They would therefore judge it worthless to sweat unduly over things, letting themselves be governed by chance. This belief has gained more credence in our own time due to the great changes that have been seen, and are still seen every day, things beyond human credibility. Sometimes when thinking about this, I am partially inclined to agree with their view. Nonetheless, in order that our free will should not be extinguished, I consider it possible that fortune is arbiter of half of our actions, but that even she leaves us to govern the other half. For she resembles one of those ruinous rivers which, when raging, floods the plains, destroys trees and buildings, and displaces earth from one place setting it down in another. Everyone flees before it, everybody submits to its impetus without being able to oppose it at any stage. And although this is the nature of rivers, it does not mean that men cannot make provisions during quiet times, by building both embankments and dykes so that when the waters rise they either run into a canal or their impetus is checked and less harmful. The same thing happens with fortune, for she shows her power where there is no force [*virtù*] marshalled to resist her, directing her impetus where she knows there are no embankments and dykes to contain her. And if you examine Italy, which is the heartland and originator of these changes, you will notice that it is a country without embankments and without a single dyke. But if she were protected by sufficient strength and wisdom [*virtù*], like Germany, Spain and France, either this flood would not have caused the changes that it has, or it would not have happened at all. I want this to be all that is said in general terms on the subject of resisting fortune.

But focusing my attention more specifically, I maintain that today one can observe a prince prospering one day and ruined the next without having seen him change his nature or character at all. I believe this arises primarily for the reasons laid out at length above, namely, that the prince who relies wholly on fortune is ruined as fortune changes. I also believe that the one who adapts the way he acts according to the quality of the times succeeds, in much the same way as the person whose way of proceeding is out of step with the times is unsuccessful. For men proceed differently in relation to the pursuit of their aims: namely glory and riches. Some proceed cautiously, others impetuously; some violently, others artfully; some with patience and others with its opposite. All of them can achieve their aims via these different methods. It can also happen that of two cautious men, one achieves his aim and the other does not, and similarly two men can be equally successful having followed different policies, one being cautious and the other impetuous. This is solely the result of the nature of the times which either does or does not conform with their way of proceeding. What I have said is based on this observation, that two people proceeding differently can achieve the same result, while of two people who proceed in the same manner one achieves his aim and the other does not. This also causes a variation in what is considered good, for if the times and circumstances evolve in such a way that a man's policy of governing with caution and patience is good, he continues to succeed. But if the times and circumstances change he will be ruined, because he fails to alter the way he proceeds. Nor will you find a man so prudent that he knows how to accommodate himself to this fact, partly because you cannot alter your natural inclinations, and also partly because when a person has prospered by following one path, you cannot persuade him to leave it. The cautious man, therefore, cannot act impetuously when the times demand it of him, and this leads to his ruin. Yet if he could change his nature according to the times and circumstances, his fortunes would not change.

Pope Julius II proceeded impetuously in all his

affairs, and found that the times and circumstances so conformed to his way of proceeding that he always met with success. Consider the first campaign he launched, against Bologna, during the lifetime of Giovanni Bentivoglio. The Venetians did not approve of it, neither did the King of Spain. When he was still negotiating about the campaign with the French, he nonetheless personally launched that campaign through his own ferocity and energy. This move caught the Spanish and Venetians undecided and inactive, the former through fear, the latter because of their desire to recapture the Kingdom of Naples. On the other hand the Pope dragged the King of France in his wake, for the King seeing his move and, desiring to make an ally of him in his attempt to reduce the Venetians' power, judged that he could not deny Julius his troops without openly harming him. With his impetuous strategy, therefore, Julius accomplished what no other Pope, with the utmost human prudence, could ever have accomplished. For if Julius had waited until all his plans were completed and everything sorted out before leaving Rome, as any other Pope would have done, he would never have succeeded, because the King of France would have made a thousand excuses and the others would have planted a thousand fears in the King's mind. I will leave all

Julius's other actions aside as they were all similar and equally successful for him, for it was the brevity of his life which prevented him from experiencing otherwise. If times had changed, however, and required him to proceed with caution, he would have been ruined. Nor would he ever have changed the way he acted as dictated by his character.

I conclude, therefore, that as fortune changes, and as men are set in their ways, they are happy so long as they get along together, and unhappy when they disagree. I consider the following very true: that it is better to be impetuous than cautious, because fortune is a woman, and it is necessary to beat her and maul her when you want to keep her under control. It is noticeable that she allows herself to be won over more by these types of men than by those who proceed dispassionately. Therefore, as a woman, she is always a friend of young men, because they are less cautious, more brutal and command her with more boldness.

XII

An Exhortation to Seize Italy and Free her from the Barbarians
(*Exhortatio ad capessendam italiam in libertatemque a barbaris vindicandam*)

Having considered, therefore, all the matters discussed above, and personally thought about whether the current times in Italy are conducive to honouring a new prince, and whether the raw material exists which would give a prudent and able [*virtuoso*] prince the possibility of imposing some form which, in turn, might honour him and benefit the people of Italy at large, it seems to me that so many things are combining to the advantage of a new prince that it is difficult to imagine a more appropriate time to act. And if, as I said, a precondition of seeing the personal ability [*virtù*] of Moses was that the people of Israel were enslaved in Egypt, and that the greatness of Cyrus was recognised because the Persians were oppressed by the Medes, and the excellence of Theseus on account of the desperation of the Athenians, in the same way, in order to recognise the strength [*virtù*] of an Italian spirit, it is necessary that Italy is reduced to her current state: more servile than the Hebrews, more abject than the Persians, more scattered than the Athenians, headless, disordered, beaten, plundered, rent, overrun and having tolerated every kind of ruination.

And although a few have shown glimmerings of hope in the recent past, encouraging us to believe that they might have been ordained by God to redeem Italy, it has subsequently transpired that they have been spurned by fortune at the height of their endeavours. Consequently, Italy remains almost lifeless, waiting to see who may be the one to heal her wounds, put an end to the sacking of Lombardy, to the ransom of the Kingdom of Naples and Tuscany, and treat her injuries which have already been festering for a long time. Mark how she implores God to send someone who can redeem her from these barbarous cruelties and abuse. See how she is also well prepared and ready to follow a standard, so long as there is someone who will bear it. Nor can she hope in anyone at present more than your illustrious house, which, with its fortune and ability [*virtù*], and the support of God and the Church – which it currently heads – can lead her to salvation. This will not be very difficult if you call to mind the actions and lives of those mentioned above. And although they were exceptional and outstanding men, they were nevertheless men, and each 58 had less opportunity than exists at present. Their undertaking was no more just than this one, nor easier, nor was God more of an ally to them than he is to you. There is great justice in this cause: 'for war is just for those to whom it is necessary, and arms are sacred when there is no hope except in arms'. There is even greater readiness, and where there is great readiness there is no great difficulty, so long as your house aims to follow the methods used by those that I have put before you. Moreover, extraordinary events are seen here, events without precedent, carried out by God: the sea is divided; a cloud has shown you the road; the rock has poured forth water; manna has fallen from the skies; everything has conspired to your greatness. The rest must be done by you. God does not want to do all things, so as not to deprive us of free will and the part of that glory that belongs to us.

It is not surprising that none of the previously mentioned Italians has been able to achieve what is hoped for from your illustrious house, and that in the course of so many upheavals in Italy and so much warfare it always seems that Italy's military vigour [*virtù*] has been spent. This happened because its ancient military provisions were not good, and there was nobody who knew how to draw up new ones. And nothing brings a man who is recently come to power more honour than the new laws and the new 59 institutions he devises. When these things are well founded and bear the mark of greatness he becomes venerated and admired. In Italy there is no lack of matter on which to impose any form. Here there is great strength [*virtù*] in the limbs, but it is lacking in the heads. See how this is reflected in duelling and skirmishes where the Italians are superior in strength, in agility and invention. But when it comes to armies, there is no comparison. This all results from the weakness of the heads, because those who do understand are not obeyed. Everyone thinks they understand although nobody to date has known how to rise up, either through their own abilities [*virtù*] or through fortune, and dominate the others. Consequently, during so much time, and so many wars fought over the past twenty years, whenever there has been an army composed wholly of Italians, it has always failed when tested, as witnessed by the battles of Taro, then Alessandria, Capua, Genoa, Vailà, Bologna and Mestre.

If your illustrious house, therefore, wants to follow those outstanding men who liberated their lands, it is necessary, above all else, to furnish yourself with the true foundation of every undertaking: your own armies. For you cannot have more faithful, more genuine and better soldiers. And although each of them is good in his own right, they will become better joined together when they see themselves led by their own prince, and honoured and maintained by him. It is necessary, therefore, to prepare these arms in order, with Italian strength [*virtù*], to defend ourselves against invaders. And although both the Swiss and Spanish infantry are considered formidable, they none-theless both have weaknesses which would allow a third force not only to withstand them but also to be confident of beating them. The Spanish cannot repel cavalry and the Swiss need to be fearful of the infantry when they encounter any as stubborn as themselves. Hence it is seen, and experience shows, that the Spanish cannot sustain French cavalry, and the Swiss are ruined by the Spanish infantry. And although there is no clear example of this latter case, nonetheless there was some indication of it during the battle of Ravenna, when the Spanish infantry confronted the German battalions, who use the same formations as the Swiss. In this instance the Spanish, using their physical agility and the help of their bucklers, passed under the German pikes and were safe in attacking them, while the latter had no means of defence. And if it had not been for the cavalry charging them, they would have killed all the Germans. So, having recog-nised the defects of both the Spanish and Swiss infantry, you would be able to form a new kind of infantry which could withstand the cavalry and not be afraid of the infantry. This would be achieved by using the right kind of weapons and altering the battle formations. These are the things which, newly instituted, grant a new prince esteem and greatness.

This opportunity must not be allowed to pass if Italy, after such a long time, is to see her saviour. Nor can I express with what love he would be received in all those provinces which have suffered from these foreign floods, with what thirst for revenge, with what resolute faith, with what devotion and tears. What doors would be closed to him? Which people would deny obedience to him? What jealousy would stand in his way? Which Italian would refuse him homage? Everyone thinks this barbarian tyranny stinks. May your illustrious house, therefore, assume this undertaking, with that courage and that hope which belong to all just causes, so that, under your standard, this country may be ennobled and under her protection the saying of Petrarch be fulfilled:

> prowess [*virtù*] against rage
> will take up arms, the combat being short:
> for ancient valour
> is still not dead within the Italian heart.